MR. FUNNY
and the Magic Lamp

Roger Hargreaves

D0544458

Original concept by
Roger Hargreaves

Written and illustrated by
Adam Hargreaves

EGMONT

Mr Funny lives in a teapot.

A teapot house.

How ridiculous I hear you say, but it suited Mr Funny right down to its spout.

Now, one day last spring, Mr Funny discovered an old trunk in his attic, which is under the lid.

And in the trunk he found a carpet.

A carpet that gave him a surprise.

For it was a magic carpet. A magic flying carpet.

Mr Funny was very excited.

There and then he decided to go on a trip to see where the magic carpet would take him.

So on that spring morning he set off on an adventure.

Mr Funny flew over Lazyland, where he woke up
Mr Lazy with a very loud raspberry and a funny face.

Mr Lazy laughed so much he fell out of bed.

Mr Funny and his magic carpet flew over Fatland, where Mr Funny made Mr Skinny laugh.

He laughed so much he tripped over a daisy and dropped the breadcrumb he was carrying for his picnic lunch.

And they flew over Coldland, where Mr Funny made
Mr Sneeze laugh.

He laughed so much that he stopped sneezing!

The magic carpet flew on and on.

They flew over mountains and valleys and over the sea.

Finally, they arrived in a desert.

But there was nobody there. Nobody to laugh at Mr Funny's funny faces.

Then, just as he was about to leave, Mr Funny saw something half buried in the sand. It was a lamp.

"What a grubby old lamp," he said to himself and he gave it a rub.

Suddenly, with a clap of thunder and in a cloud of smoke, a genie appeared in front of Mr Funny.

Which was all very exciting, but what Mr Funny noticed most of all was how miserable the genie looked.

Mr Funny had never seen anyone look so unhappy.

"Master," said the genie, glumly, "I am the Genie of the Lamp and I appear before you to grant you three wishes."

To the genie's surprise, Mr Funny pulled one of his famous funny faces.

But the genie did not laugh.

He did not chuckle.

He did not even smile.

Not a flicker.

"Oh dear," said Mr Funny. It was going to take a bit more than a funny face to cheer up this genie.

And then he had a thought.

"For my first wish, I wish for a piano-playing elephant."

"As you command, Master," said the genie, and then before you could say 'broken piano stool' a piano-playing elephant appeared before them.

Mr Funny roared with laughter.

It was hilarious!

But it was not funny enough to make the genie laugh.

He looked just as glum as before.

Mr Funny had another thought.

"For my second wish, I wish for a mouse."

And before you could say 'squeak' a mouse appeared.

And as Mr Funny and you probably know, great big elephants are frightened of teeny tiny mice.

The elephant trumpeted in fear and jumped on top of the piano, which broke under the elephant's weight.

Mr Funny laughed with delight.

"Now, that was funny," chuckled Mr Funny.

"Not really," said the genie, who looked just as unhappy as before.

"You are a gloomy fellow," said Mr Funny.

"You would be too," said the genie, "if you had to live in that lamp!"

"It must be a tight squeeze," admitted Mr Funny.

"You can say that again," grumbled the genie. "There's no room even to cough living in a lamp."

"I live in a teapot. A very comfortable teapot, mind you," said Mr Funny, and then yet another thought struck him.

"For my third wish, I wish your lamp was a house."

And before you could say 'bring me a builder' the Genie's lamp had turned into a house!

The genie smiled.

Only a flicker of a smile, but at least a smile.

"That's more like it," said Mr Funny. "Now, how am I going to get this elephant back home? I know! I wish …"

"I'm sorry," interrupted the genie. "You've used up your three wishes."

So Mr Funny and the elephant had to squeeze on to the magic carpet for their ride home. It was quite a sight.

Rather funny, in fact.

So funny, the genie roared with laughter!